THE AMERICAN GIRLS

 KAYA, an adventurous Nez Perce girl whose deep love for horses and respect for nature nourish her spirit

1764

1774 **FELICITY**, a spunky, spritely colonial girl, full of energy and independence

1824 **JOSEFINA**, a Hispanic girl whose heart and hopes are as big as the New Mexico sky

1854 **KIRSTEN**, a pioneer girl of strength and spirit who settles on the frontier

1864 **ADDY**, a courageous girl determined to be free in the midst of the Civil War

1904 **SAMANTHA**, a bright Victorian beauty, an orphan raised by her wealthy grandmother

1934 **KIT**, a clever, resourceful girl facing the Great Depression with spirit and determination

1944 **MOLLY**, who schemes and dreams on the home front during World War Two

1774
HAPPY BIRTHDAY,
Felicity!
A Springtime Story

BY VALERIE TRIPP

ILLUSTRATIONS DAN ANDREASEN

VIGNETTES LUANN ROBERTS, KEITH SKEEN

★ American Girl™

Published by Pleasant Company Publications
For information, address: Book Editor,
Pleasant Company Publications, 8400 Fairway Place,
P.O. Box 620998, Middleton, WI 53562.

Visit our Web site at **americangirl.com**.

Printed in China
05 06 07 08 09 LEO 25 24 23 22 21

PICTURE CREDITS
The following individuals and organizations have generously given
permission to reprint illustrations contained in "Looking Back":
p. 63—Frog in the Middle, from *Kate Greenaway's Book of Games*, Michael O' Mara Books, Ltd.;
pp. 64–65—Abby Aldrich Rockefeller Folk Art Museum, Williamsburg, VA; DAR Museum,
Washington, DC; Colonial Williamsburg Foundation (rattle, walker); pp. 66–67—Colonial
Williamsburg Foundation (baby's gown and stays, pudding cap); Abby Aldrich Rockefeller
Folk Art Museum (portrait of two children); pp. 68–69—The Corning Museum of Glass,
Corning, NY; Courtesy, American Antiquarian Society (young woman with
spinning wheel); Colonial Williamsburg Foundation.

Library of Congress Cataloging-in-Publications Data

Tripp, Valerie, 1951–
Happy birthday, Felicity! : a springtime story / by Valerie Tripp ;
illustrations, Dan Andreasen ; vignettes, Luann Roberts, Keith Skeen. — 1st ed.
p. cm. — (American girls collection)
Summary: As her tenth birthday approaches, Felicity is excited by her
grandfather's visit, but she is also concerned about the growing tensions between
the colonists and the British governor in Williamsburg.
ISBN 1-56247-032-9 — ISBN 1-56247-031-0 (pbk.)
[1. Virginia—Social life and customs—Colonial period, ca. 1600-1775—Fiction.
2. Family life—Fiction. 3. Williamsburg (Va.)—Fiction.]
I. Andreasen, Dan, ill. II. Title. III. Series.
PZ7.T7363Han 1992 [Fic]—dc20 91-33527 CIP AC

TO ANN, BOBBY, KATIE, AND SARAH

TABLE OF CONTENTS

FELICITY'S FAMILY
AND FRIENDS

FATHER
*Felicity's father,
who owns one of the
general stores in
Williamsburg*

MOTHER
*Felicity's mother,
who takes care of
her family with love
and pride*

FELICITY
*A spunky, spritely
colonial girl, growing
up just before the
American Revolution*

NAN
*Felicity's sweet and
sensible sister, who is
six years old*

WILLIAM
*Felicity's three-year-old
brother, who likes mischief
and mud puddles*

GRANDFATHER
*Felicity's generous
grandfather, who
understands what is
important*

BEN DAVIDSON
*A quiet apprentice
living with the
Merrimans while
learning to work in
Father's store*

ELIZABETH &
ANNABELLE COLE
*Elizabeth, Felicity's
best friend, and her
snobby older sister,
Annabelle*

MISS MANDERLY
*Felicity's teacher—
a gracious gentlewoman*

ISAAC WALLACE
*A brave drummer for
the militia*

SPRINGTIME PROMISES

Felicity opened the kitchen window as wide as it would go and leaned toward the sunshine. The wind still had a whisper of winter in it. But the sun shone strong with the promise of springtime, and the sky was a clean, clear blue.

It was spring cleaning day at the Merrimans'. Felicity was in the kitchen scrubbing the big silver chocolate pot in a tub of sudsy water. Nan and William were helping her. That is, William was *supposed* to be helping. He was supposed to wash the wooden stirrer that went with the chocolate pot. Instead, William was using the stirrer as if it were a drumstick. He was happily hitting the

water to make it splash up out of the tub.

Outside the kitchen window, Felicity could see Mother and Rose airing mattresses from all of the beds in the household. They leaned the mattresses against the kitchen garden fence to freshen them in the bright spring sunshine.

Felicity spoke to her mother through the open window. "Mother," she said, "since Grandfather will be here with us on my birthday this year, do you think we might have a little party?"

Mrs. Merriman smiled at Felicity. "What sort of party?" she asked.

"Well," said Felicity as she thought, "it would be a small party. Just our family and Ben. It would be a celebration—a celebration of all of us being together and of spring." Felicity talked faster as her ideas poured out. "We could decorate the parlor with flowers. Grandfather loves flowers. I am sure tulips and daffodils will be blooming in my garden by then. We could use my favorite plates and our best chocolate cups. Oh! And we could have a fancy cake on the glass pyramid and—"

"Tarts!" interrupted Nan.

"Tarts and tarts and tarts!" added William.

"Yes, indeed," agreed Felicity. "Peach, blackberry, and raspberry tarts."

Mother laughed. "Lissie," she said, "you are always ahead of yourself. Your thoughts run off and away like wild ponies! You know 'tis days till Grandfather comes and weeks till your birthday." She helped Rose lift and turn one of the mattresses. "It's hard to believe you will be ten this year, Lissie," she said, "though you do grow fast as a weed. Perhaps that's what comes of being born in the spring."

"I like having a birthday in the spring," said

Felicity. "Everything is blossoming and growing. The whole world is starting life new."

"Aye," agreed Mrs. Merriman. "The springtime suits you. You were born sooner than I expected. You couldn't wait to be born and start life new, as you say." She laughed. "You have been impatient and in a hurry ever since! Grandfather will be amazed to see how tall you've grown."

"Me, too," William said stoutly. "I'm taller, too!"

"Oh, much taller!" said Felicity. "We have lots of changes to show Grandfather. He hasn't even met Ben yet!" Ben was the apprentice in Mr. Merriman's store.

A small frown crossed Mrs. Merriman's face. Felicity realized her mother was afraid Ben might speak out in front of Grandfather. Ben did not think the colonies should belong to the King of England anymore. But Grandfather was a strict Loyalist. He would not take kindly to anyone who criticized the king!

Felicity looked down at the silver chocolate pot. She gently rubbed it dry. "Do you think Grandfather will be angry that we don't drink tea anymore?" she asked her mother. To protest the tax the king had set on tea, Mr. Merriman had stopped selling tea in his store, and the Merrimans had stopped drinking tea at home. "Will Grandfather mind drinking hot chocolate instead?"

Mrs. Merriman shook off her troubled look. "No one would mind chocolate poured from such a shiny pot!" she said cheerfully. "Now take off your wet apron. 'Tis time for you to go to your lessons at Miss Manderly's. Don't forget to stop at the house and fetch your hat. This spring sun will burn your nose quite pink!"

"Yes, Mother," said Felicity. She unpinned her apron and handed it to her mother. Then she skipped up to the house to tidy herself for lessons.

Felicity's best friend, Elizabeth, was waiting for her at the pasture behind the Wythes' stable. They often met there before lessons to visit the Wythes' mare and her new colt. Elizabeth was standing on the bottom rung of the fence watching the horses across the pasture. When she saw Felicity, Elizabeth smiled. "Oh, good. Here you are, Lissie," she said.

"Do whistle and make the horses come to us."

Felicity whistled. The mare trotted toward her, and the colt followed behind like a little, shy shadow. Elizabeth and Felicity pulled up handful after handful of sweet spring grass and fed it to the horses.

Felicity giggled, "The colt's tongue is so wet and rough, it tickles my hands." She wiped her hands with her handkerchief, but they were still rather sticky and quite green from the grass.

"I do love to visit those horses," Felicity said later. She and Elizabeth were giving their hands a quick wash at the Wythes' well. "They make me think of my horse Penny. I hope Penny has not forgotten me."

Elizabeth's big blue eyes were serious. "Penny has not forgotten you," she said. "You saved her from that mean Mr. Nye, who beat her. You were patient with her. You taught her to trust you. Now you must trust *her*. Trust that she still loves you. Trust that she will come back to you if she can. Someday she will. I am sure."

6

Felicity smiled at her friend. Elizabeth always spoke straight from her heart.

The girls hurried along to their lessons. When they came into Miss Manderly's sunny parlor, they saw that Elizabeth's older sister, Annabelle, was already there, looking very prim. Annabelle put on a pained expression when she saw them. She sniffed, then held her handkerchief to her nose. Felicity grinned. She supposed she and Elizabeth must smell a tad horsey after their visit to the pasture.

"Good day, young ladies," said Miss Manderly. "Please be seated at the table. I have set up your needlework frames. Work quietly while Annabelle has her music lesson."

"Yes, Miss Manderly," said Elizabeth and Felicity. They sat at their needlework frames, facing each other across the table.

Felicity had finally finished her sampler of stitches at the end of the winter. When Miss Manderly said she was ready to move on to more difficult stitchery, Felicity was very pleased. She

loved the wooden needlework frame that sat so
prettily on the table in front of her. The frame held
the linen taut while she made her stitches.

A gentle spring breeze played with the leaves
outside the window. They seemed to dance with
the soft music Miss Manderly was strumming on
Annabelle's guitar. When Miss Manderly began to
sing, it seemed to Felicity that the sound filled the
room with color and light.

Then Miss Manderly handed the guitar to
Annabelle. Oh no! Felicity and Elizabeth looked at
each other and tried not to groan. For now it was
Annabelle's turn to play and sing.

Horrible sounds filled the room and chased
away all the beautiful music. When Annabelle played,
the guitar sounded whiny, tinny, and twangy. And
her singing was even worse.

*"In spite of all my friends could say, young Colin
stole my heart away,"* warbled Annabelle.

"Indeed, I wish someone would steal *all* of her
away," Elizabeth whispered. "She sings as if her
stays are laced too tight."

Felicity laughed softly. But secretly, she was
envious of Annabelle. She wished with all her heart

*"I wish somebody would steal **all** of her away," Elizabeth whispered.*
"She sings as if her stays are laced too tight."

she were old enough to learn to play the guitar. But she knew young ladies did not begin music lessons until they were twelve or thirteen years old.

Felicity looked at Annabelle's guitar out of the corner of her eye. It was made of shiny wood, shaped like half a pear, with a long, slender neck. Felicity hated to admit it, but Annabelle looked grown-up and elegant when she held the guitar. Felicity longed to strum the guitar and to touch the luscious satin ribbon Annabelle had tied to it.

When at last Annabelle stopped singing and -playing, Felicity went over to her. "Annabelle," she asked, "may I hold your guitar?"

"Oh, dear me, no!" said Annabelle. She held the guitar closer to her. "Papa just bought this guitar. It was very costly. You are far too, too . . . you simply may not touch it!"

Felicity flushed.

Miss Manderly said, "I am sure Felicity will be careful, Annabelle."

Felicity started to hold out her hands. Annabelle pulled back as if she'd seen a snake. "Gracious me!" she exclaimed. "Look at your hands! They are *green!* They are filthy!"

Felicity glanced at her hands and then quickly hid them behind her back. They were only the tiniest bit grass-stained. They were *not* filthy. "I beg your pardon," Felicity said in a cold voice. She turned on her heel and stalked back to her chair. Snippy Annabelle! She could *keep* her precious guitar.

CHAPTER
TWO
—
POSIE

Morning after morning, the spring
days burst into beauty like blossoming
flowers. Morning after morning, Felicity
worked hard to prepare her garden for Grandfather's
inspection. He was due to arrive any day now.
Felicity wanted her garden to look perfect for him.

Grandfather had taught Felicity many things
about gardening. He believed gardens should be
orderly, well kept, and useful as well as beautiful.
That is why Felicity had vegetables and herbs
growing in tidy rows next to her flowers.

Felicity loved to feel the rich, dark earth so cool
and heavy in her hands. It smelled of sun and rain.
The little seedlings pushed up out of the earth, first

as a soft green fuzz and then as slender, budding stems. Each flower was different. Each was determined to stand up and offer its face to the sun. But weeds wanted to grow, too. There was one weed in particular that was especially stubborn. No matter how many times Felicity dug out its tough green stem, the spiky weed came back.

"I think you had better let that weed grow," said Ben. He was leaning over the garden fence, grinning at Felicity. "You can't seem to discourage it."

Felicity grinned back at Ben. "I don't truly mind it," she said. "Indeed, I rather like it. 'Tis so stubborn. But I know Grandfather would not approve. And I want Grandfather to think my garden is in fine order."

"Well," said Ben. "Things that grow have a will of their own. 'Tis hard indeed to stop them." He stuck the stem of the weed in his buttonhole. Suddenly, Ben stood up straight. He called out, "Good day, Isaac!"

Isaac was a free black just a little older than Ben. He and his family did laundry work at their home on the edge of town. Several times a month, Isaac came to the Merrimans' house to pick up laundry to be washed or to return clean laundry.

Isaac came toward Felicity and Ben. He set down the laundry basket. "Good day to you," he said with a smile. "Felicity, your garden is fine indeed!"

"Thank you, Isaac," said Felicity.

"Isaac," said Ben earnestly. "You are a drummer with the militia, aren't you?"

"Aye," answered Isaac. "That I am."

"Will you teach me how to play beats on your drum?" asked Ben.

"Me, too?" asked Felicity.

"Very well," said Isaac. "I don't have my drum with me now. But I can give you both a quick lesson anyway." He picked up two sticks from the ground and held them as if they were drumsticks.

"The drums are very important to the militia," Isaac explained. "They tell the soldiers what to do. Different drumbeats mean different things. This beat tells everyone to wake up." Isaac beat a loud, insistent beat on the garden fence. *Rat tat TAT! Rat tat TAT!* "And this beat tells the men to come quickly and line up with their guns." Isaac played a louder beat. *Brrrrump pum pumpety! Brrrrump pum pumpety!* "And this beat is my favorite. It's called 'roast beef.' It means dinner is ready." Isaac beat a lively roll. *Pumpety pumpety pumpety pum!*

Isaac gave Ben the sticks, and Ben tried playing the beats. Then Felicity had a turn. "You do well, Felicity," Isaac smiled.

Ben glanced at Felicity. Then he said to Isaac in a low voice, "I made a delivery to the Raleigh Tavern yesterday morning. I heard a rumor that Governor Dunmore has the key to the Magazine, where all the colonists' gunpowder is stored. They say the governor wants to have his marines take all the gunpowder away."

Magazine

Felicity spoke up, "But if the governor's men took our gunpowder, that would be stealing. Why would the governor do such a thing?"

Isaac looked at her gravely. "The governor is afraid," he said. "He knows the colony's militia is practicing more often. He is afraid the colonists will use the gunpowder in the Magazine to fight against him and the British soldiers. He fears the time is coming when the colonists will fight for their independence."

"But the governor isn't a *thief*," insisted Felicity. "He wouldn't *steal*."

Isaac said softly, "A frightened man may do anything."

Ben sighed. "Lissie, things have changed a great deal since you went dancing at the Governor's Palace in January," he said. "The king has sent more and more British troops here. It looks as if the British are getting ready to fight. Relations between Loyalists and Patriots have grown much worse. Many people are beginning to distrust the governor because he is the king's representative here."

Felicity shook her head. She said, "I am *sure* . . . "

"Nothing is sure, when trust is gone," said Ben.

Felicity hoped Ben wouldn't say anything in front of Grandfather about people distrusting the governor. Grandfather would be terribly displeased.

The very next afternoon, Felicity floated home
from lessons humming the minuet Miss Manderly
had played on Annabelle's guitar that day. She
danced into the stable yard,
then stopped. Marcus was
unharnessing a horse from a
dusty riding chair. She knew
that riding chair. It belonged to Grandfather!

"Grandfather!" Felicity shouted happily as she
ran into the parlor.

There he was, standing with Father, brushing
the dust off his coat.

Grandfather made Felicity an elegant bow.
"Good day," he said formally. "Do I have the honor
of addressing Miss Felicity Merriman? The young
lady who attended a dance lesson at the royal
Governor's Palace?"

"Oh, Grandfather!" laughed Felicity as she
hugged him. "I am so glad you are here. I must tell
you all about the dance at the Palace. 'Twas very
fine! And there's a new colt at the Wythes', and you
must see my garden, and . . . "

"Did you plant the herbs and vegetables near
the kitchen as I told you, and the sweet-smelling

flowers nearest the house?" Grandfather asked.

"Aye!" said Felicity. "Everything is growing nicely, but there is one weed that is so stubborn it will not go away."

"Stubborn, you say?" said Grandfather. "Let's go have a look at it. Perhaps I know its name and how to tame it."

"Now, Father," said Mrs. Merriman as she carried in a pitcher of cool water to drink. "You just arrived. Are you not hot and tired?"

"Aye!" said Grandfather with a smile. "So the garden is the very place for me. No place is more refreshing than a garden, eh, Felicity?"

Felicity nodded happily and took his hand.

"And," said Grandfather, "there's someone outside Felicity must meet."

"Oh, very well," laughed Mrs. Merriman. "Go along with you!" She and Mr. Merriman smiled as Felicity and Grandfather hurried out into the sunshine.

Grandfather was a tall, spare gentleman who stood very straight. He wore no wig, but instead tied his white hair back in a queue. His soft gray eyes were usually full of gentle good humor.

Felicity skipped next to Grandfather,
wondering whom she was to meet. Just
as they reached the garden gate, William
ran up to her and pulled her by the hand.
"Come, Lissie! See what Grandfather has
brought us!" he cried. "Look!"

queue

In a far corner of the garden, Felicity saw Nan
holding what looked like a lapful of soft white fluff.
Suddenly, the fluff bleated! Felicity hurried toward
Nan. She knelt and looked into the small, sweet
face of a lamb.

"Ohhhh," sighed Felicity. "Ohhhh! What a dear!
Oh, Grandfather! I've never seen such a love!" The
lamb looked at Felicity with big, gentle eyes. Felicity
patted the lamb's soft fleece. "Is the lamb ours?"
Felicity asked. "May we care for her?"

"Well," said Grandfather slowly. "I believe it is
a good thing for children to have animals to care for.
It reminds them that they are not the only living
creatures on the earth. But taking care of an animal
is a big responsibility. Do you think I can trust you
to raise this lamb properly?"

"Oh, yes!" said Nan, William, and Felicity all
at once.

"Oh, Grandfather!" sighed Felicity. "I've never seen such a love!"

Grandfather smiled. "Very well then," he said. "If you do a good job, the lamb may stay here. But if I see that you are irresponsible, I shall take the lamb back to my farm. Is that fair?"

"Yes!" said Nan and William.

"Thank you, Grandfather," said Felicity. Nan put the lamb in Felicity's lap. Then she and William ran off to tell Mother and Father about Grandfather's gift.

Grandfather sat down on the bench next to Felicity. "I know this little lamb won't replace your Penny," he said. "But perhaps she can be a comfort to you."

Felicity smiled at Grandfather. She hugged the lamb gently. "Thank you, Grandfather," she said again. "Thank you."

Nan and William came back, dragging Mother and Father with them.

"See the lamb, Mother?" said Nan. "See how little she is?"

"What will you call your new pet?" asked Mother.

Felicity laughed as the lamb stood on its shaky legs and wobbled right into the middle of some flowers. "I think we should call the lamb Posie," Felicity said, "because that will remind us of where she will be if we don't keep an eye on her!"

GRANDMOTHER'S GUITAR

Spring kept its promise of beautiful days. Huge white clouds sailed across the gloriously blue sky. The apple trees were heavy with pink blossoms, and the air was sweet with their delicious scent.

Felicity loved being with Grandfather. Elizabeth did, too. She joined them in the garden almost every day before lessons. Grandfather sat in the shade with Posie at his feet. He watched Felicity weed, water, and prune her plants. Elizabeth made miniature landscapes out of the cuttings. She used twigs and stems for trees and moss for grass. Buds and petals were her flowers, and leaves were her ferns.

One afternoon, Grandfather studied Elizabeth's landscape closely. "What place have you made here?" he asked. "This is a miniature of a real garden, is it not?"

"Oh, 'tis my garden at home—I mean, in England," answered Elizabeth.

Grandfather nodded. "You miss it, do you?" he asked.

"Aye," said Elizabeth. "My family came here to Virginia in the fall. This is my first spring away from England."

Felicity sat back on her heels and looked at Elizabeth. She had never heard Elizabeth speak this way before. She had never thought about Elizabeth missing England.

Grandfather spoke thoughtfully. "I grew up in England, too," he said to Elizabeth. "I, too, was transplanted to the soil of another country. 'Tis not easy to feel at home in a new place."

Elizabeth sighed. "You see, sir, my parents are Loyalists," she said. "And some people here have different ideas. They say the colonies should not belong to the king anymore. 'Tis hard to know what to think."

"Humph!" snorted Grandfather. "All this talk against the king and his governor is stuff and non-sense! 'Tis the ranting of irresponsible scoundrels. The colonies are part of England and will be so forevermore."

Felicity looked at Grandfather's stern face. *It's a good thing he did not hear Ben and Isaac talking about the governor,* she thought. She went back to her digging.

Felicity did not want to hear any more disturbing talk about the king and England. But it seemed to follow her like an unwelcome, bothersome fly. That evening, after supper, Ben went off to visit a friend. After Ben left, Grandfather frowned.

"You had better keep an eye on that young man," Grandfather said to Father. "He is much too interested in the militia. He'll be shirking his duties at the store to sneak off and watch them muster if you don't stop him."

"Ben is a good lad," said Father. "I trust him."

"Humph!" said Grandfather. "How can you trust someone you know is disloyal to the king? I heard Ben say the colonies should be independent.

These young Patriots talking about rebellion know nothing about trust or loyalty. They have forgotten that loyalty is a promise to honor our old and valuable traditions."

"Aye, sir," said Father. "We must honor traditions. But perhaps we must honor new ideas, too."

"Balderdash!" sputtered Grandfather. "New ideas are new nonsense! People are nothing if they are not loyal to their old values and traditions. They are irresponsible—"

"Now, now," interrupted Mrs. Merriman. "Please let us have no arguing and disharmony. I hope there is room in the world for old ideas *and* new ideas, just as there is room for, for . . ." She looked around the room and smiled when she saw the spinet. "Just as there is room for old songs and new songs." She sat at the spinet and started to play. "Let us sing together."

Felicity could see that Grandfather was still cross. But he and Father were gentlemen, so they politely joined in the singing. And soon enough, the music soothed and cheered everyone.

"Felicity, my dear," said Grandfather. "You have a fine voice. I think perhaps you have your grandmother's gift for music. I have brought something for you. Wait here."

He left the room for a short while. When he came back, Felicity could hardly believe her eyes. Grandfather handed her a guitar! A beautiful, graceful guitar! It was made of the same shiny wood as Annabelle's guitar, but Felicity thought it was much finer. It had a flower carved in the middle where Annabelle's guitar had only a hole.

Felicity hardly dared to touch the guitar. She looked up at Grandfather and asked, "Is this . . . is this for *me?*"

"Aye," said Grandfather. "It belonged to your dear grandmother. You must promise to be very careful with it." He glanced at Father and said firmly, "It is old and valuable, and so it is something to be treasured."

"Indeed, yes," said Mrs. Merriman quickly. "We shall keep the guitar in the house, in the parlor, where it will be safe."

Felicity cradled the guitar in her arms. She felt as if she had been given something magic, something full of enchanting music waiting to come out, waiting for *her* to bring it out. She brushed the strings with her fingertips. They were out of tune, and the fine old ribbon tied to the guitar was frayed. But to Felicity the guitar was perfection. It *was* a treasure.

"Thank you, Grandfather," she said. "I promise to take good care of the guitar. Someday, when I am older, I'll play it for you. We'll sing together."

Grandfather's eyes were their softest gray. "Indeed we shall, my dear girl," he said. "I know you will guard it well and keep it from harm. You are a young lady to be trusted."

Later that night, when she was lying in bed, an idea wormed its way into Felicity's thoughts. *Now I have a guitar,* she realized. *I have a guitar that is finer than Annabelle's. How I wish I could show it to her!* Felicity quickly reminded herself that Mother had said the guitar must be kept in the parlor so that it would be safe. She was not to take the guitar out of the house. So Felicity tried to push the idea away. But somehow, it would not go.

Days passed, and soon it was April twentieth, the day before Felicity's birthday. That afternoon,

"I know you will guard it well and keep it from harm," Grandfather said. "You are a young lady to be trusted."

Mother, Nan, William, and Grandfather went to
visit old Mr. Fitchett. They left before Felicity
went to lessons, and they were not due back until
early evening.

After Felicity waved good-bye to them, she
wandered into the parlor and took the guitar
down from the tall bookcase. She plucked the
strings. *'Tis too bad the guitar is so out
of tune,* she thought. She tried to
tighten the strings herself, as she
had seen Miss Manderly do when
she was tuning Annabelle's guitar.
But she did not know how the notes were supposed
to sound. Felicity put the guitar back in its place.
She stared up at it.

Perhaps, she thought, *perhaps Miss Manderly
would tune the guitar for me. And perhaps Miss
Manderly could teach me a song to play at our party
tomorrow! That would be a fine surprise for everyone.
Surely Mother and Grandfather would not mind if
I took the guitar out of the house for such a good purpose.
Indeed, I should think they would be pleased.*

But in her heart, Felicity knew Mother and
Grandfather would not be pleased if she took the

guitar without asking. And in her heart she knew the real reason she wanted to bring the guitar to Miss Manderly's house. She wanted Annabelle to see it. She wanted to make Annabelle jealous.

Quickly, before she could think more carefully, Felicity took the guitar down from the bookcase again. Her hands were cold as she carried it out the door and along the street. She had a sickly feeling in the bottom of her stomach that she was doing something wrong, but she walked briskly to her lessons, as if she could leave the feeling behind her.

Elizabeth gasped when Felicity entered Miss Manderly's parlor. "Oh, Lissie!" Elizabeth exclaimed. "You brought your Grandmother's guitar, the guitar you told me about. It *is* beautiful!"

Felicity knew Annabelle was staring at the guitar as she handed it to Miss Manderly. "My grandfather gave me this guitar," Felicity said proudly. "I was wondering if you might tune it for me?"

Miss Manderly smiled. "I should be pleased to," she said. "This is a fine old instrument, Felicity." She tuned the strings and then strummed a few chords. "Hear the depth of sound it has. Such a rich tone!" She handed the guitar back to Felicity. "Guard this well," she said. "It is a work of art."

"Felicity," said Annabelle in a sweet voice. "I did not bring my guitar today. May I hold yours? I will show you how to play a tune."

"Thank you, Annabelle," Felicity said politely. "But I think Miss Manderly and I must be the only ones to hold the guitar. 'Tis very old and very precious. I promised to be most careful with it."

"Indeed!" said Annabelle. She looked at the guitar again with a little pout on her face. Then she looked away.

Felicity turned to Miss Manderly. "Would you teach me to play a little, Miss Manderly?" she asked. "Just a chord or two, or a short tune?"

Felicity held the guitar, and Miss Manderly placed her fingers on the strings. It was more difficult to make music than Felicity had thought, but she tried very hard. And the old guitar seemed eager to sound beautiful.

"You have a good ear and a firm touch, Felicity," said Miss Manderly. "When you are old enough for serious lessons, you will do well."

Annabelle pretended not to hear, but Felicity knew she was listening because her pout grew poutier. When lessons were over, Annabelle flounced out ahead of Elizabeth and Felicity. Felicity smiled to herself. *Annabelle is envious of my guitar!* she thought. Felicity was pleased. She had forgotten about the sickly feeling in her stomach.

DRUMBEATS

After lessons, Felicity and Elizabeth said good day to Miss Manderly and followed sulky Annabelle outside. Elizabeth had invited Felicity to spend the afternoon at her house. Mrs. Cole, Elizabeth and Annabelle's mother, greeted them at the door in a flutter of confusion.

"Girls, girls, girls," she said. "Do be quiet! Your father has some very important visitors. British military men! Officers!"

"Officers?" said Annabelle, perking up. "Shall I play and sing for them?" She patted her hair and fluffed her petticoats.

"Oh, dear me, no!" exclaimed Mrs. Cole. "No, you must be quiet as mice. Go to your rooms. Or better yet, go out to the garden, won't you?"

"Humph!" exclaimed Annabelle. She swept up the stairs to her bedchamber in a huff.

Felicity and Elizabeth happily went outside and sat on a bench under the leafy arbor. Felicity played the tune Miss Manderly had taught her. The guitar sounded even lovelier outside in the spring air. Elizabeth hummed along. After a while, she wandered about the garden, picking flowers. Felicity played on and on. What a pleasure it was to play the guitar!

"Lissie," Elizabeth called. "Do come here and tell me the names of these flowers. They are such a pretty pink."

Felicity leaned the guitar against the bench. She skipped over to join Elizabeth and look at the flowers. "Those flowers are called sweet William," Felicity said. "But somehow they do not quite remind me of my brother William. They are so pink and proper, and he is usually so muddy!"

Elizabeth laughed. "Let's pick some," she said, kneeling down. "We can use the blossoms to make a flower necklace for Posie and pompons to put in *our* hair."

"Oh, that is a fine idea," agreed Felicity, joining her. The two girls picked small handfuls of sweet William. Then Felicity asked, "Do you have any violets? They would look lovely in your fair hair."

"I think there are violets growing in front of the house," said Elizabeth.

"Let's go look," said Felicity. She and Elizabeth walked around to the gardens in front of the house. Suddenly, Felicity heard the low rumble of drums. "Listen!" she said. "Do you hear the drums? The militia must be mustering on the green."

"What does *mustering* mean?" asked Elizabeth.

"Mustering is when the men in the militia get together to practice marching and shooting and following orders," explained Felicity. "Come! Let's go watch."

"I don't think I want to," said Elizabeth. "Let's go see Posie."

"We'll see Posie *after* the muster," said Felicity impatiently. She grabbed Elizabeth's hand and pulled her out the front gate, along the street, and across Market Square to the green next to the Magazine. A large crowd had gathered to watch the men muster.

Felicity and Elizabeth wove their way through the crowd until they found Ben. Ben grinned when he saw Felicity. "I knew you'd come when you heard the drums," he said. He pointed to the drummers. "Look. There's Isaac."

Felicity saw Isaac with his drum. Just then the fife players began to pipe a sharp, lively tune. Isaac and the other drummers beat upon their drums. The men shouldered their guns and marched in rows behind the drummers. Little boys ran alongside, shouting with excitement. The men marched smartly across the green, in step with the drumbeats, their guns glinting in the sun. Felicity felt the drumbeats thunk in her stomach. The fife music gave her goose bumps on her arms. And when the men stopped, turned, and fired their guns into the air, Felicity's heart jumped.

fife and drum

"Oh!" exclaimed Elizabeth beside her. "Let's go *home!*"

Felicity turned to her in surprise. "But it's so exciting!" she said.

Elizabeth looked miserable. "I think it's scary,"

The men marched smartly across the green, in step with the drumbeats,
their guns glinting in the sun.

she said. "I'm going. Good-bye." She ran off before Felicity could say another word.

Felicity soon forgot everything as she stood next to Ben, watching and listening. She tried to name the drumbeats Isaac and the other drummers were playing. She counted the rows of men and studied the horses the officers rode. She sniffed the air. It was heavy with smoke and dust and the burnt tang of gunpowder.

Felicity felt proud of the militia men. "They look fine, don't they, Ben?" she said. "I know the men in the colonists' militia are just citizens and not paid soldiers like the king's soldiers. But they do look fine today."

Ben was so intent watching the muster that Felicity thought he did not hear her. His arms were folded across his chest, and his eyes were wide.

Then he nodded. "The militia has been practicing more often since March," he said. "Militias in every county in Virginia have been practicing more. We have to be ready to defend ourselves."

"In a fight against the king's soldiers?" asked Felicity.

"Aye," said Ben.

Suddenly, it struck Felicity. Suddenly, she realized why Elizabeth was frightened. These men were not practicing just to make excitement. They were practicing to get ready to fight and to die if they had to. And whom would they have to fight? They would fight soldiers, real soldiers, British soldiers, the best soldiers in the world. These men might die because they did not want to be ruled by the King of England anymore. They were ready to give their lives to be independent. Then the argument against the king would no longer be about drinking tea or not drinking tea. It would be a matter of life and death. Felicity shivered. This time it was not a shiver of excitement. It was dread.

Clouds covered the sun. As the muster was dismissed, a soft rain began to fall like a chilly veil. Felicity and Ben walked home quietly.

"I wish more than anything I could join the militia like Isaac," said Ben. "I'd give anything to be able to fight." His voice was full of longing.

Felicity looked over at him. "But you cannot join the militia, Ben," she said. "You are an apprentice. Apprentices are not allowed to join.

'Tis in your agreement with Father. Is it not?"

"Aye," said Ben in a low voice. "I cannot join the militia as long as I am an apprentice. But . . . "

"Ben!" Felicity said sharply. "You wouldn't break your agreement with Father! He trusts you! You'd never run away, would you? You *couldn't*."

Ben looked at her and said nothing.

Felicity burst out. "You are our friend, Ben! You are part of our family. It wouldn't be honorable to run away."

Ben gave Felicity a sad grin. "I won't do anything while your grandfather is here," he said. "Your grandfather would be furious."

"Aye," said Felicity. "Grandfather has strict ideas. He . . ." Suddenly Felicity stopped stock still. "Oh no! Oh *no!*" she cried. "Grandfather! The guitar! Oh, Ben! I forgot! I *forgot!* I left the guitar at Elizabeth's house!" Felicity grabbed Ben's arm with both hands and spoke quickly. "I must run to the Coles' and get the guitar. If Mother and Grandfather are home, tell them I am on my way! But don't tell them about the guitar! They will be angry."

"Aye!" said Ben. "Run! Run fast!"

Felicity took off as fast as her feet could go. Her heart pounded as she ran through the gray drizzle. If only she could sneak the guitar back home before Mother and Grandfather returned. Oh, how she wished she had not been so thoughtless!

Felicity was a fast runner. In a few minutes, she reached the Coles' house. She ran back to the garden and hurried toward the arbor where she had left the guitar. Ah! She panted with relief. There it was, propped against the bench just where she had left it. But when Felicity reached for the guitar, she saw someone coming. It was Mr. Cole and a British officer. Felicity did not want them to see her, so she ducked behind a bush. She hugged the guitar to her chest.

The British officer was speaking in a serious voice. "The governor's marines are about five miles away, at Burwell's Landing on the James River," said the officer. "They'll come very late tonight and take the gunpowder out of the Magazine."

Felicity froze. She could not believe her ears.

The officer went on, "Governor Dunmore will tell the people of Williamsburg that he heard rumor

of a slave uprising. He'll say the gunpowder was removed for the colonists' own protection."

Mr. Cole spoke up. "The people will know that's a lie. They will know the governor has stolen their gunpowder," he said. "Everyone knows the governor is afraid the colonists will use the gunpowder to fight against him and our British soldiers. 'Tis sad indeed when the governor must stoop to such low deeds as lying and stealing."

The officer sounded angry. "I beg your pardon, sir!" he said.

"Aye," said Mr. Cole. "We must all beg pardon

for what the governor is about to do. This will destroy any last shred of trust the colonists have in him. I am loyal to the king, but I am sorry to be involved in such deeds." He sighed. "Very well, then," he said to the officer. "You may go. I have received your report."

The two men walked away, but Felicity did not move. The British officer's words echoed in her head. *The marines are going to take the gunpowder tonight!* She had to tell someone! They must be stopped! What on earth was she going to do? What could she possibly do?

Felicity ran home holding the guitar close to her. She was full of fear and confusion.

When Felicity stepped into the house, her heart sank. Mother, Father, and Grandfather all sat in the parlor. Felicity put the guitar behind her back.

Mrs. Merriman looked up with a smile. "There you are, Lissie," she said. "Were you playing with Posie? We shall . . . " She stopped. The smile faded from her face. "Felicity, what is the matter? You look a fright! And what do you have behind your back?" Mrs. Merriman came over to Felicity. "Why, it's the guitar," she said as she took it away. "And

just look at it! The ribbon is torn through! The guitar
is wet! Felicity! What *have* you done?"

Felicity could not meet her mother's eyes. "I'm
sorry. Truly I am. I meant no harm," she said. "I just
wanted Miss Manderly to tune it and . . . and I wanted
Annabelle to see it."

"You took the guitar?" asked Mother. "But you
were most clearly told not to take it out of this house.
And how did it get so wet?"

"Well, I . . . it was a mistake," said Felicity. "I was
playing it at Elizabeth's house, and then we went to
the muster, and I . . . I forgot it."

Felicity hung her head. She had never felt so
ashamed in her life.

Mrs. Merriman looked angry and sad at the same
time. She handed the guitar back to Felicity. "Show
your grandfather what you have done. You must ask
him to forgive you," she said.

Felicity slowly carried the guitar to Grandfather.
Her eyes filled with tears. "I'm sorry, Grandfather,"
she whispered. "Please forgive me. I am so sorry."

Grandfather took the guitar and touched the
bedraggled ribbon. He frowned. "I was wrong to
bring the guitar here," he said. "I see now that you are

too young to be trusted with something so valuable."

"Go to bed, Felicity," said Father. "Think about what you have done."

Felicity started to go. She wanted to run from the room, run from the house, and never face any of them ever again. But she made herself stop and turn around. "Father," she said. "Please listen to me."

Mr. Merriman nodded. "What is it?" he asked.

Felicity took a deep breath. "When I went back to the Coles' house to fetch the guitar just now, I heard Mr. Cole talking to a British officer. The officer said . . ." Mother, Father, and Grandfather were frowning at her, but Felicity forced herself to go on. "The officer said British marines would come tonight to take the gunpowder out of the Magazine. And Mr. Cole said it was stealing, but . . ."

"Stop!" growled Grandfather. His eyes were dark as thunderclouds. "Stop this wild talk! 'Tis foolish, irresponsible, shameful! Stop it, I say!" He shook his head in anger. "Felicity, I am sorely disappointed in you. Sorely!"

Felicity was rigid with shame.

Father sighed. "Felicity, how can you expect

us to believe such a tale?" he asked. "You have shown yourself to be dishonest and irresponsible in the matter of the guitar. How can we possibly trust you?"

"But Father," Felicity said, "I did hear them! I did!"

Father held up his hand. "Don't disgrace yourself further by spreading wild falsehoods, especially about such serious matters," he said sternly. "Go now. We have heard enough from you for one evening."

THE LONG, DARK NIGHT

Felicity gave up. She trudged up the stairs to her bedchamber. She had never felt so miserable in her life. She threw herself on her bed and wept bitterly.

Felicity cried until she had no more tears. Then she sat by her window, watching the rain fall softly, silently, until the sky was dark. She wished with all her heart she had not taken the guitar. She wished she had not left the guitar at Elizabeth's house. Most of all, she wished she had not heard Mr. Cole and the officer talking. The burden of what she had heard them say was too heavy for her to bear. She wanted to forget it. But she could not. She knew she had to tell someone about the plan to steal the gunpowder. There were only two people who could help her—Ben and Isaac.

Felicity waited until she could no longer hear the deep murmur of voices from the parlor. When the house was quiet, and everyone else was asleep, she tiptoed out of her room.

Down the stairs she went without making a sound. She hurried out the door, across the yard, and to Ben's room above the stable. When Felicity got to Ben's door, she found it was closed tight and latched. How could she wake him? If she called to him, she'd wake Marcus and the horses. Felicity had an idea. With her finger, she tapped the drumbeat Isaac had taught her. *Rat tat TAT! Rat tat TAT! Rat tat TAT!* Once, twice, three times she tapped the beat that meant *wake up!*

It worked. Ben opened the door. "Lissie!" he gasped. "What is it? What—"

"Shhh!" cautioned Felicity. "Listen! It's *tonight*, Ben. The marines are coming to steal the gunpowder tonight. I heard an officer say so when I was at the Coles'. Come quick! We've got to wake Isaac. We need his drum."

Ben looked dazed. "Lissie . . ." he began.

"Come *now!*" hissed Felicity impatiently. "We have no time to waste!"

Ben nodded. He pulled on his coat and followed Felicity out of the stable. Quiet as cats, they ran through the eerie darkness.

At the street corner, Felicity stopped. "You go to the Magazine," she said to Ben. "The marines may be there already. Shout as loud as you can if you see anything. I'll go get Isaac."

"Aye," said Ben. He disappeared.

Felicity hurried on. The sky was so clouded,  she felt as if she were swimming through black water without a single star to guide her. Alone, she ran through the deserted town, past the back streets, to Isaac's house. Felicity knew Isaac and his brother slept in a shed attached to the back of the house. She crept up to the door and rattled it.

"Isaac!" she whispered. "Isaac! Wake up!"

Isaac opened the door a crack. "Felicity!" he said. "What's the matter?"

"Come with me. You've got to," said Felicity.

"The marines are going to steal the gunpowder *tonight*. Ben is already at the Magazine, keeping watch. You must come and bring your drum to sound the alarm."

Isaac looked hard at Felicity. "It is very dangerous for a black person like me to be seen on the streets in town at night," he said. "If I were found . . ." He shook his head. "It would not go well for me."

"I know," said Felicity. "But you must trust me, Isaac. We've got to stop them from stealing the powder. Please. You must help."

Isaac didn't say another word. He picked up his drum and drumsticks, grabbed a cloak, and followed Felicity.

They found Ben crouched against the brick wall that surrounded the Magazine. "Nothing yet," he whispered. "And look. There's no guard here tonight. Someone is definitely up to no good."

Isaac, Ben, and Felicity huddled together in the rainy darkness. Isaac covered himself and his drum with his cloak. Hour after hour, they waited. The night became colder, wetter, and blacker. They heard nothing. They saw nothing.

51

"It is well past midnight," whispered Isaac.

Felicity was too cold and too frightened to be tired. Doubt began to creep into her mind, cold as the chill from the rain. Over and over, she repeated to herself what she had heard the officer say to Mr. Cole. *The governor's marines are about five miles away, at Burwell's Landing on the James River. They'll come very late tonight and take the gunpowder out of the Magazine.* She had not misunderstood, had she? She *couldn't* be wrong.

Ben shifted restlessly and sighed. Isaac accidentally knocked his foot against his drum. *Clunk!* Then, a moment later: *Clunk!* Felicity tensed. She held her breath. *Clunk!* There it was again! That was the unmistakable sound of a cart. *Clink!* That was the sound of a harness. Then Felicity heard footsteps. Ben and Isaac looked at her. They heard the sounds, too.

"Lift me up so I can see," whispered Felicity.

She stood on their shoulders and peeked over the top of the wall surrounding the Magazine. By the light of a lantern, men were loading barrels of gunpowder onto a cart. They worked quickly and quietly, their shoulders hunched against the rain.

By the light of a lantern, men were loading gunpowder onto a cart.

Felicity slipped to the ground. "The marines are in there! They are loading the gunpowder onto a cart!" she said. "Beat your drum, Isaac! Beat it as loud as you can!"

Isaac flung back his cloak. He pulled the drum strap over his shoulder and began to pound on his drum with all his might. *Brrrrump pum pumpety! Brrrrump pum pumpety!* The drumbeats crashed like thunder. The marines shouted in surprise. *Brrrump pum pumpety! Brrrrump pum pumpety!* The Magazine seemed to shake with the force of the drumbeats. Isaac's strong arms pounded and pounded his drum. *Brrrrump pum pumpety! Brrrrump pum pumpety!*

Felicity could hear the marines calling out to each other and clambering into the cart. The whip snapped, the horse whinnied wildly, and suddenly the cart rumbled out the gate of the Magazine and down the street, as fast as it could go.

Brrrump pum pumpety! Brrrrump pum pumpety! Still Isaac beat on. Ben and Felicity ran from house to house, beating on the doors, banging on the windows. They shouted as loud as they could, "Make haste! Come quick! The marines have stolen our gunpowder! Hurry!" And all the while Isaac beat his drum. *Brrrrump pum pumpety! Brrrrump pum pumpety!*

Windows flew open. People poured out of their houses carrying burning torches. They ran to the Magazine, shouting to one another in wild confusion. In no time, a mob had gathered. Their faces were angry in the fiery torch light. Their loud voices filled the night with noise, drowning out the beat of Isaac's drum.

"They've stolen our gunpowder!" voice after voice cried. "It's gone!"

"The governor will answer for this!"

"This is thievery! Villainy! Our gunpowder is gone!"

"The governor's behind this! He must pay!"

Felicity could feel anger sweep through the crowd of people. Isaac caught her eye and nodded. Then he slipped away to go home. Felicity and Ben sank out of the circle of torch light. Felicity was suddenly weary. She was glad when she saw Father's face coming toward her through the blur of the crowd.

"Felicity!" said Father. "Ben! What on earth are you two doing here?"

"We sounded the alarm, sir," said Ben to Mr. Merriman. "We saw the marines stealing the gunpowder, and we sounded the alarm." His voice was proud.

Felicity lifted a tired face to her father. "I had to do it, Father," she said. "I know you will be angry. But I had to do it."

Mr. Merriman put his arm around Felicity's shoulders. "Come along now," he said. "Both of you. It is dangerous here. You belong at home."

Ben, Father, and Felicity walked home, leaving the fiery torches, the noise, and the confusion behind them.

When Felicity woke the next day, her room was so full of sunlight she knew it was long past  noon. *Today is April twenty-first. It is my birthday,* she realized. *I am ten years old today. I wonder if it will be a happy day.* She stared at the bright path the sunshine made on her floor and thought about the dark events of the night before.

Felicity could hear the muffled bustle of her family going about household chores below her. Then her door opened a crack. Father looked in.

"Ah, you are awake," he said.

Felicity sat up. "Father," she said. "What happened? Did they catch the marines? Did they bring the gunpowder back?"

"No," said Father. "All is quiet now. The crowd was angry, though. The people marched over to the Palace early this morning to see the governor. They demanded that the governor return the gunpowder or pay for it." Mr. Merriman sighed. "But even if he does make amends, I am afraid none of us will trust the governor ever again. Nothing will be the same after the incident at the Magazine last night. Nothing will ever be the same."

"Father," said Felicity, "will you trust *me* again? Will you and Mother and Grandfather ever trust me again?"

"Well," said Mr. Merriman, "you made a terrible mistake, taking the guitar. But you made no mistake about the incident at the Magazine. You told the truth, and you acted bravely. I think you have earned back our trust."

"Will Grandfather forgive me?" asked Felicity.

"You will have to ask him that yourself," said Father. "All of this business has been very hard on your grandfather. He feels a great loyalty to his king, but he has lost faith in Governor Dunmore. He thinks the governor was wrong to have taken the gunpowder. 'Tis hard for an honorable gentleman like your grandfather when he loses his trust in someone he once respected." Mr. Merriman kissed Felicity's forehead. "Dress and come down to the parlor," he said as he left.

Felicity put on her pretty pink gown and pinned a flowered apron over it. Grandfather would like the little posies on it. The spring sunshine had lit a tiny hope in her. Perhaps spring's promise of the world starting anew would be true for her, and she could start anew with Grandfather. Perhaps Grandfather *would* forgive her.

When Felicity walked into the parlor, she smiled in delight. Her whole family and Ben were gathered around the table, smiling back at her.

"Oh . . . oh, it's enchanting!" Felicity gasped

as she looked around the room. The parlor was transformed. Huge bunches of flowers made the room look like a garden in bloom.

At the center of it all was the table with Felicity's favorite plates and the glass pyramid laden with a cake and tarts. The silver chocolate pot gleamed like a mirror. It was surrounded by Mother's very finest pale yellow cups with their fancy handles. Felicity felt as if she were looking at a dream.

Mother kissed Felicity gently. Then she fastened a pompon of pretty pink, blue, and white flowers to Felicity's hair ribbon. "This is for you, my dear girl," she said, "with wishes for great happiness on your birthday."

"Thank you, Mother," said Felicity. She kissed her mother's cheek.

Grandfather came forward carrying the quintal vase filled with colorful flowers. In the center of the vase, Grandfather had placed the stubborn weed from Felicity's garden. It had blossomed into bright pink flowers. Felicity smiled when she saw it. Grandfather smiled, too.

"Aye, 'tis your weed," he said. "I decided something that is so determined to grow must be respected. And I think someone as brave as you must be forgiven a mistake."

Felicity hugged him as hard as she could.

"You were born this day ten years ago," Grandfather went on. "And with your birth began a joy unlike any other we'd ever known. We want to celebrate the joy you bring us, Felicity."

Grandfather reached into his pocket. He pulled out a long, wide, silk ribbon of a deep, shimmering red. "This is to replace the old ribbon on your guitar," he said. "I have decided that you should keep the guitar. I am sure you will treasure it now more than ever."

Felicity could hardly speak for happiness. "Oh, I will, Grandfather," she said. "I will."

LOOKING BACK

GROWING UP
IN
1774

This portrait of a sleeping baby was painted by an unknown artist in the early 1800s.

In colonial times, a family of five people, like Felicity's, was rather small. Many parents had eight or more children. Usually, though, several of these children died before reaching adulthood.

Embroidered pincushions were popular baby gifts in Felicity's day.

A colonial baby rattle with bells, a whistle, and a piece of polished coral for teething.

In fact, almost half of all children died before the age of six. Colonial people did not understand the importance of eating proper food to stay healthy or of keeping clean to avoid germs. Many children died from diphtheria, whooping cough, smallpox, or other diseases that today's doctors know how to prevent or treat.

Babies were born at home. The birth was usually attended by a *midwife*—a woman who helps mothers during childbirth—as well as female relatives and servants. After a baby was born, a woman like Felicity's mother stayed in bed for a week or more. She rested for up to a month to get her strength back. Slave women and other working mothers usually could not rest for so long. Today, most women are active soon after their children are born.

Parents usually had their babies *christened* a few weeks after birth. Christenings were religious ceremonies, attended by relatives and close friends, that often included feasting and dancing.

Some babies learned to walk standing in the center of "walkers" like this.

While they were babies, both girls and boys were dressed in loose-fitting gowns. Later, when they were William's age, they wore dresses called *frocks*. Under their gowns or frocks, some young boys and girls from

A colonial baby's gown and stays

families like Felicity's wore tightly laced *stays*. Parents believed the stays improved posture and provided back support. Even babies wore stays!

By the age of five or six, girls began dressing more like their mothers, while boys were *breeched*. Breeching meant that boys no longer wore frocks and stays but instead began to wear pants called *knee breeches*. This change symbolized boys' break from the female world. From that time on, fathers took a greater role in teaching their sons, while girls continued to follow their mothers' example closely.

Some young children wore **pudding caps** *to protect their heads during falls as they learned to walk.*

The child at the left is a boy dressed in a frock.
He is holding his pet, a tamed squirrel.

Colonial children, even wealthy ones, didn't have
as many toys as most children in the United States do
today. Felicity and her friends had fun playing charades
or singing games, going for walks or horseback rides,
playing musical instruments, and reading aloud. If an
eighteenth-century Virginia child did have a toy, it was
usually handmade. Wealthier parents might buy their
child an imported doll or set of toy soldiers.

How a child's teenage years were spent depended
on the family's position in the community. Children from
laboring families were already working long hours each
day, helping their parents or working for other families
in kitchens, fields, or shops. Boys from wealthier families

were still in school or, like Ben, were apprenticed to learn a trade Girls from wealthier families had usually finished their education in reading and writing. They continued to improve the "skills of housewifery" needed to manage a home.

Young men and women began to learn the skills they would need as adults.

Girls and boys met and courted at dances, teas, and other entertainments. The parents of young people hoped that their children would choose mates who were from the same kind of family as they were. Girls usually married in their late teens and soon began families of their own.

Boys reaching the age of 16 were required to begin practicing with the militia, unless they were black or under contract as apprentices. The militia was a group of men who had to be ready to fight and defend their city or county if it was in danger. Between the ages of

12 and 16, whites and free blacks, like Isaac, could serve as drummers or fifers for the militia.

The Williamsburg militia kept its guns and equipment in the Magazine, a military storehouse. The raid of the Magazine by British marines, which you read about in *Happy Birthday, Felicity!*, actually happened. Nobody knows for certain who raised the alarm that stopped the soldiers from taking more of the colonists' gunpowder out of the Magazine, but it could have been young people like Felicity, Ben, and Isaac. The event angered many colonists who wanted independence from England, and it helped lead to the Revolutionary War.

Williamsburg's Magazine stored weapons, gunpowder, and other equipment for the militia.

A Sneak Peek at

Felicity

Saves the Day

*Grandfather is buying some new horses! As Felicity
gazes at them, her heart skips a beat.
One of them looks familiar . . .*

The dining room was hot and stuffy, and Mrs. Wentworth's words only made it worse. Felicity knew she should sit still and appear to be interested in the conversation even though she did not like what Mrs. Wentworth was saying. But her feet were jumpy, and her legs itched. There was sand stuck in her stockings. Felicity put her hands through the slits in her gown and petticoat as if she were reaching into her pockets. She slipped her hands past her pockets, untied her garters, and put them in her pockets. Then she jiggled her legs so that her stockings fell down around her ankles. Ah, now, *that* felt better!

"Gracious!" said Mrs. Wentworth suddenly.

Felicity realized Mrs. Wentworth was looking at her.

"Felicity!" Mrs. Wentworth puffed. "You are as twitchy as a cat's tail! What ails you, child?"

Quickly, Felicity put her hands up on the table. "Well, I . . ." she began.

Grandfather rescued her. "May I ask you ladies to excuse the gentlemen?" he asked. "Mr. Wentworth has brought some horses for me to look at. And I would like Felicity to join us. I shall need her advice.

"Felicity!" Mrs. Wentworth puffed. "You are as twitchy as a cat's tail!
What ails you, child?"

She has quite an eye for a good horse."

"Oh, yes, of course!" said Mother. Mrs Wentworth nodded.

Felicity was so grateful to be going, she forgot about her stockings. They flopped around her ankles as she followed the gentlemen out of doors and down the path to the pasture behind the stable. The sun was scorching hot. Still, it felt wonderful to be out of doors.

Felicity took a deep breath. She loved the stable smell of horses and sun-warmed hay. She stood next to Grandfather and looked over the pasture fence at the five horses Mr. Wentworth had brought. Most of the horses stood quietly in the shade of the stable, nibbling at the grass. Felicity shaded her eyes to better see one horse that was at the far end of the pasture, trotting restlessly along the fence.

"These are cart horses," Mr. Wentworth said to Grandfather. "Some of them are handsome enough to pull your riding chair. The others are steady and strong. You won't find a better horse than one of these to pull a farm wagon."

"They appear to be in fine condition," said Grandfather. "Let's have a closer look." He opened the gate and led Felicity and Mr. Wentworth into the pasture. The stable boys looped ropes around the horses' necks and led them to Grandfather one by one. Grandfather inspected the horses carefully. He ran his hands down their legs and looked at their eyes and teeth to be sure the horses were healthy.

Suddenly, there was an uproar. The horse at the far end of the pasture whinnied, and kicked up its heels, and ran wildly. It would not let the stable boy near enough to put the rope around its neck.

Mr. Wentworth shook his head. "That horse was passed along to me in a swap and I took her, for she's a Thoroughbred," he said. "She's handsome, and fast as the very wind. But she's very skittish. I fear she was once so badly mistreated, she trusts no one."

The horse reared up, and Felicity gasped. She slipped past Grandfather and ran toward the horse as fast as she could.

"Stop!" Mr. Wentworth shouted. "Stop! That horse is dangerous!"

The horse was skinny and scruffy and so covered with dust that her coat was the color of mud. She tossed her head and danced from side to side. Felicity made herself slow to a walk as she came nearer. Her heart thudded in her chest so that she could hardly breathe.

"Penny," Felicity said softly. "Penny. It's me. It's Felicity. You remember. You remember me, don't you, Penny? Don't you, my girl?" Felicity stood still and held out her hands. "Come to me, Penny," she said. "Come, my fine one."

The horse nickered. She took one step, then two, toward Felicity. Then, very gently, she nudged

Felicity's shoulder with her nose.

Felicity's eyes filled with happy tears. She reached up and put her arms around Penny's neck. "I knew we would find each other again someday," Felicity whispered.

Felicity turned and slowly walked back toward Grandfather. Penny followed close behind her. The men stood by the stable, watching, silent. Felicity smiled at Grandfather. "This is my horse, Grandfather," Felicity said simply. "This is Penny."

READ ALL OF FELICITY'S STORIES,
available at bookstores and *www.americangirl.com.*

MEET FELICITY • An American Girl
Penny, the horse Felicity loves, is in trouble. Felicity must
figure out a way to help her before it's too late!

FELICITY LEARNS A LESSON • A School Story
Lessons about serving tea pose a problem for Felicity—
how to be loyal to her father *and* to her friend.

FELICITY'S SURPRISE • A Christmas Story
Felicity's mother becomes terribly ill. Is Christmastide
really a time when hopes and dreams come true?

HAPPY BIRTHDAY, FELICITY! • A Springtime Story
Felicity overhears a message that means danger
to the colonists, and she must warn them herself.

FELICITY SAVES THE DAY • A Summer Story
Felicity's friend Ben has run away and needs help.
Will Felicity help Ben—or tell her father where he is?

CHANGES FOR FELICITY • A Winter Story
Felicity faces many changes in her friendships
and her family as war breaks out in the colonies.

◆

WELCOME TO FELICITY'S WORLD • 1774
American history is lavishly portrayed
with photographs, illustrations, and
excerpts from real girls' letters and diaries.

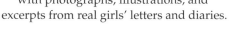